Be Bigger

Book 2
Talking with Trees Series

Written by Colleen Doyle Bryant
Illustrated by Manuela Soriani

Published in USA by LoveWell Press
Illustrations by Manuela Soriani
ISBN-13: 978-1477403754
ISBN-10: 1477403752

More about the Talking with Trees series at **TalkingTreeBooks.com**

Thanks for believing in me.

"Hmph," said the girl.

"Is something bothering you?" came a voice like a warm breeze.

"No. I'm fine. I have the whole thing figured out," the girl snapped.

Just then, she started to look around. She saw an old elm tree next to her, the school far across the playground, and not another person close enough to talk to.

“Am I talking to a tree?” she wondered aloud.

“Well I am the only one here,” said the tree with a wink. “So what’s bothering you? Kids at this school have been telling me for a long time that I’m a very good listener.”

“I don’t need to talk. I’ve figured it out. I’m just going to invite Emma’s sister over after school. But I am *NOT* going to invite Emma,” the girl said, with her arms crossed and her chin in the air.

“Why not?” asked the tree.

“Because last time I was at Emma’s house, she had another friend come too. And you know what she did? She totally ignored me! She didn’t even notice when I left!” she howled.

“Oh, I see,” said the tree.“Your feelings are hurt so you’re going to get even with Emma.”

“Getting even? I’m not getting even,” the words coming from the girl in a great rush. “I just want to play with Emma’s sister today—without Emma.”

“Usually you and Emma have lots of fun together,” said the tree.

“I guess we do,” the girl said thoughtfully. “But she hurt my feelings!”

“I understand. Your heart and your stomach are tied up in knots. If you leave Emma out so her heart hurts too, will that help you feel better?” asked the tree.

“Not when you say it like that. That just sounds mean. But what else can I do?” pleaded the girl.

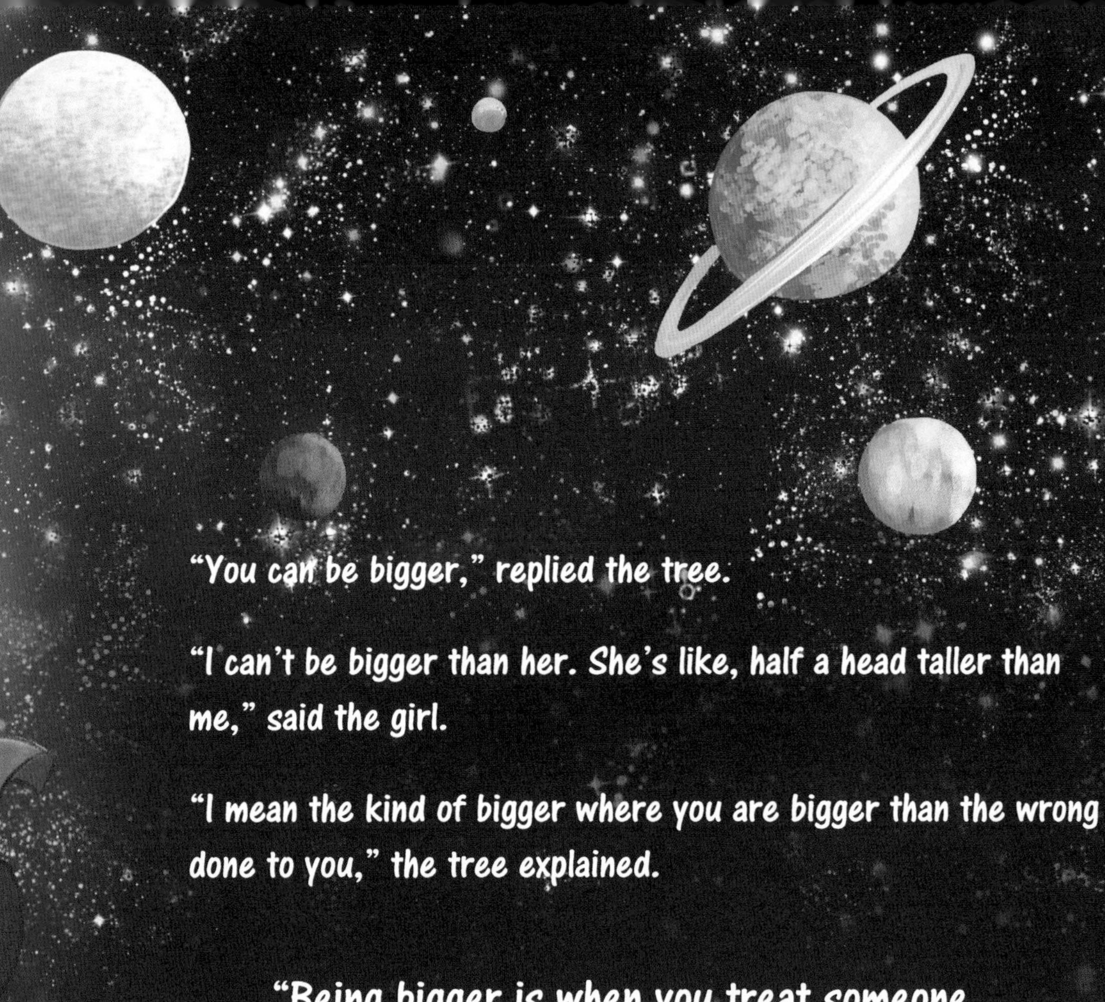

"You can be bigger," replied the tree.

"I can't be bigger than her. She's like, half a head taller than me," said the girl.

"I mean the kind of bigger where you are bigger than the wrong done to you," the tree explained.

"Being bigger is when you treat someone the way you would like to be treated, even when they haven't been that kind to you."

"Why should I be nice to her? She hurt me and I want her to know," said the girl, with her brow furrowed and her hands clenched in fists.

“Let me tell you a story about your grandmother. I saw her here one day with her arms crossed and a scowl on her face just like yours,” said the tree.

“You know my grandma?” asked the girl, curiosity winning out over her anger.

“Of course. She went to this school too, and I’ve been standing in this same spot watching kids play for a long, long time,” explained the tree.

"My grandma went to school? Here? I thought they were too busy chasing dinosaurs and stuff," said the girl with a smirk.

"Not only did they have schools, they had friends and lots of the same problems you and your friends work through," chuckled the tree.

"Your grandma had a very good friend who hurt her feelings. Your gran was so mad, she decided to ignore her friend when she came to the lunch table.

"So then her friend's feelings were hurt and she invited other girls to play jump rope, but left your gran out on purpose.

“Then your gran retaliated by not inviting her friend to her sleepover, even though all the other girls in the class were invited.

“Well you see where this is going. One hurtful action led to another, and next thing you know, your gran and Mildred were enemies,” said the tree.

“What??? Do you mean Auntie Mildred? She and Gran are best friends!” she cried, puzzled.

“They are now. But only because your gran finally decided the time had come to be bigger than the mess she was in,” explained the tree.

"How did she be bigger?" asked the girl.

"She thought about what she really wanted," explained the tree.

"First, she wanted to have her good friend back.

"She also wanted to stop the ache that was in her heart all the time. Staying mad and feeling hurt takes a lot out of you when you keep doing it every day."

"That's for sure," murmured the girl.

"Your gran went to Mildred and explained that the whole thing started because the last time she was at Mildred's house, she felt left out and ignored," said the tree.

"Mildred, feeling a bit guilty, explained that she hadn't realized your gran was upset. She apologized for not paying more attention to your gran's feelings from the start.

"Then, Mildred told Gran that she felt pretty awful when Gran ignored her and didn't invite her to the sleepover.

"They figured out that it felt a lot better to talk about how they felt than to stay in a big fight," said the tree.

easy way
right way

"That sounds awfully hard—and embarrassing. I don't want to talk to Emma. It'll be easier just to pretend nothing happened," said the girl.

"Well, there's the easy way, and there's the right way.

"If you want the ache in your heart to stop, choose the right way," advised the tree.

"Like I said, that sounds awfully hard," the girl complained.

"Sometimes doing the right thing is hard. But it's only hard for a little while, then it gets better," said the tree.

“When you pick the easy way, your heart aches with anger and regret a little bit... but you stay bummed for a long time.

“When you pick the right way, you might feel embarrassed or really uncomfortable for a short while, but then it gets better and the aches in your heart melt like chocolate on a summer day,” she said.

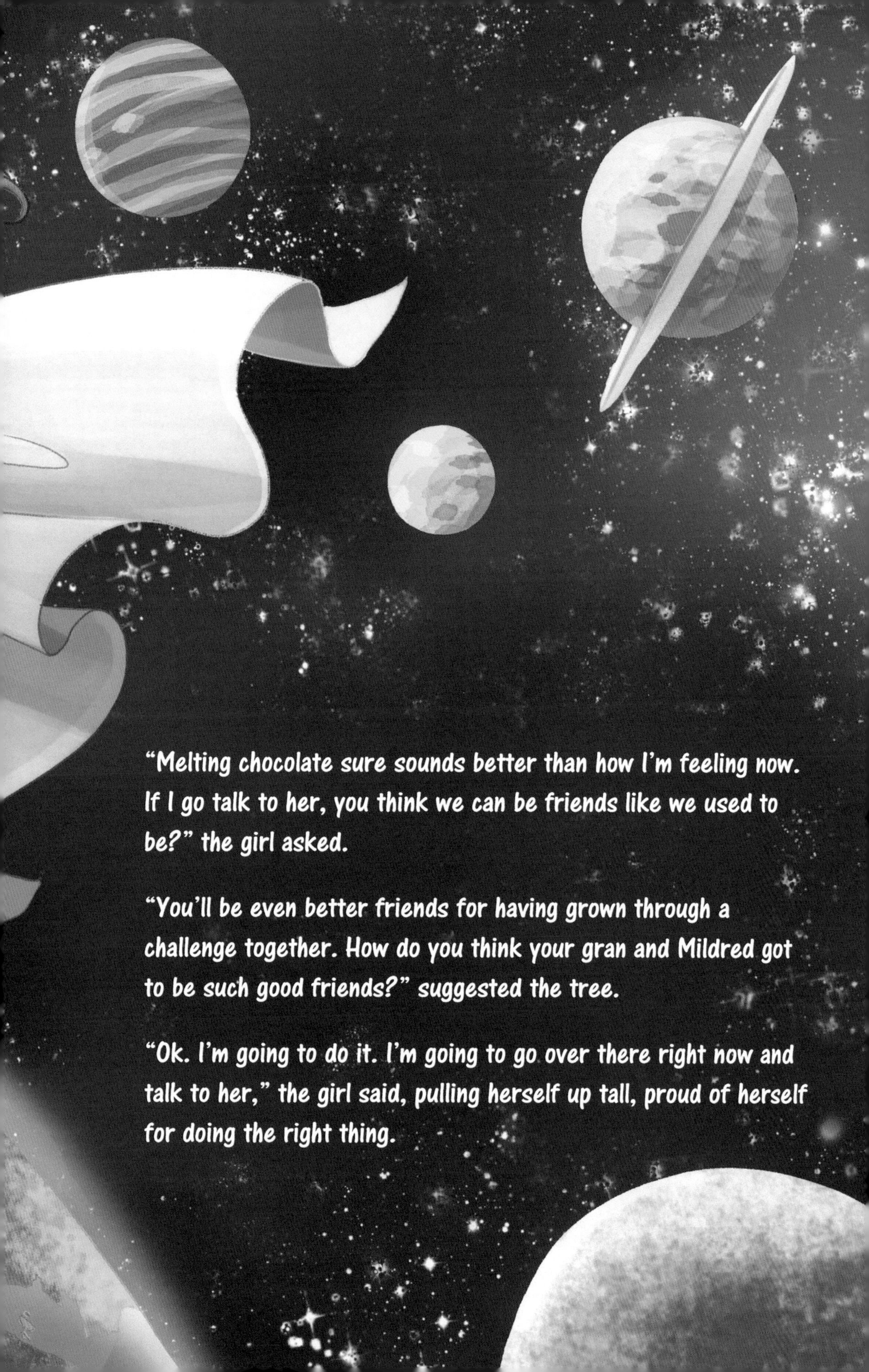

"Melting chocolate sure sounds better than how I'm feeling now. If I go talk to her, you think we can be friends like we used to be?" the girl asked.

"You'll be even better friends for having grown through a challenge together. How do you think your gran and Mildred got to be such good friends?" suggested the tree.

"Ok. I'm going to do it. I'm going to go over there right now and talk to her," the girl said, pulling herself up tall, proud of herself for doing the right thing.

I'm proud of you too...

What would you say if you could talk to a tree?

Trees make great listeners, and so do your grown-ups.
So go ahead and speak up. What are you thinking about?

The tree said to the girl, "I understand your heart and your stomach are tied up in knots." Have you ever felt that way? Why?

What does it mean to "be bigger"? Does it mean you need to grow taller or does it mean you can choose to rise above your anger and hurt to make a good choice?

In the story about the girl's grandma, we see Gran had her feelings hurt. How did she handle it? What could she have done differently?

The tree talks with the girl about choosing between "the easy way" and "the right way". Have you ever been in a situation when you could choose the easy way out, but decided to do the right thing?

How would you handle these friendship troubles?

You hear that one of your good friends said something mean about you to someone.

a. March right over to her and tell her she's not your friend anymore.

b. Go to your friend and ask if she really said it. Then let her know that it hurt your feelings for her to talk about you like that to someone else. Tell her you'd rather she talk to you if she doesn't like something you do.

c. Ignore it. It'll go away on its own.

You are surprised to find out that everyone in class got an invitation to your friend's birthday party, except for you.

a. Plan a super fun party and don't invite him. He left you out, you leave him out.

b. Tell everyone you didn't want to go to his boring party anyway.

c. Ask him if there's been a mistake. If he didn't invite you on purpose, try to work out what's wrong in the friendship.

Your friend was so rude today. She snapped at you and wouldn't share at recess.

a. Think about how nice she usually is. Ask her if she's having a bad day or if something's bothering her.

b. Forget her as a friend. Nobody treats you that way.

c. Tell all your friends how rude she was.

More from the author:

TalkingTreeBooks.com

Talking with Trees Series

More stories about honesty, respect, responsibility and forgiveness

Printable coloring pages

Online resources for parents and teachers

SuperEasyStorytelling.com

Super Easy Storytelling

Start telling stories with your kids instantly! A simple formula, story ideas, and illustrated cliffhanger stories make it easy to tell a story together—anytime, anywhere.

Home schoolers and teachers, the Super Easy Storytelling teaching tools make learning literacy fun.

ISBN: 1453630503

Made in the USA
Lexington, KY
08 July 2015